I'm a Tiger Too!

For
Diarmuid, Donnchadh
and Cian, with love.
With thanks to
Findabhair and Rousseau
for the inspiration.

First published in Great Britain in 2001 by

GULLANE
CHILDREN'S BOOKS

Winchester House, 259-269 Old Marylebone Road,
London NW1 5XJ

1 3 5 7 9 10 8 6 4 2

Text and illustrations © Marie-Louise Fitzpatrick 2001

The right of Marie-Louise Fitzpatrick to be identified as the author and illustrator of this work
has been asserted by her in accordance with the Copyright, Designs and Patents Act 1988.

A CIP record for this book is available
from the British Library

ISBN 1-86233-234-7

Printed and bound in China

I'm a Tiger Too!

Marie-Louise Fitzpatrick

GULLANE
CHILDREN'S BOOKS

"Hey, Mew!

Are you a tiger?

I'm a tiger too.

Let's be tigers together

and tumble through the jungle.

Rrroarr!

Oh, don't go!

I don't want to be a tiger all alone.

Hey, Ruff, are you a wolf?

I'm a wolf like you.

We are wolves,
big and fierce.
Let's howl at the moon

Oh, don't go!

I don't want to be a wolf all alone.

Swish, swish, Mr Fish, you and me,

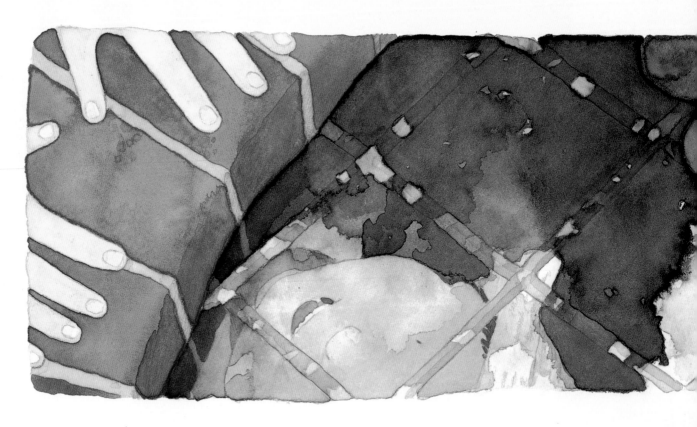

let's be sailors on the sea.

Over the waves, across the sea.
Swish, swish!

Oh, don't go!

I don't want to be a sailor all alone."

"What's going on?   Who are you?"

"I'm a boy," said the boy.   "I'm a boy like you."

"But I'm a tiger!" said
Tiger-Wolf-Sailor on the Sea.

"Will you be a tiger too?"

"I'll be a tiger," said the boy.

Rrroar!